Zack had been given a present.
He was very proud of it.

He sat in the dark. He switched it on and off, on and off, on and off.

He went out and lit things up with it: a slug, a snail, and some ants.

Then he went back to his room.

"Come and look at this!" he shouted to Jess.

He lit up a cobweb. There was a cobweb pattern on the wall.

"Cool!" said Jess.

"Wait till you see this!" exclaimed Zack.

He pointed under the bed.
Something went scuttling back
into the gloom.

“Yuck! Disgusting!” said Jess and stood up. Zack was still looking under the bed.

“If it is dark, the thing will come back,” muttered Zack. He clicked the switch off and waited.

Just then, there was a snorting sound next to him, and something wet brushed his cheek.

"Help!" he shouted.
"A monster!"

Zack shot out from under the bed. Jess was giggling. She pointed to a tail sticking out from under the bed.

Rags had come to look under the bed too.

"Thank goodness it was you, Rags, and not a monster!" said Zack.